Strega Nona's Magic Lessons

STORY AND PICTURES BY Tomie de Paola

VOYAGER BOOKS • HARCOURT BRACE & COMPANY
San Diego • New York • London

for
BARBARA LUCAS,
WHO TAUGHT ME
SOME MAGIC LESSONS
OF HER OWN. t.deP.

Voyager Books is a registered trademark of Harcourt Brace & Company.

Library of Congress Cataloging-in-Publication Data
dePaola, Tomie.
Strega Nona's magic lessons.
"Voyager Books."
Summary: Big Anthony disguises himself as a girl
in order to take magic lessons from Strega Nona.
[1. Magic—Fiction.] I. Title.
PZ7.D439St   [E]   80-28260
ISBN 0-15-281785-9
ISBN 0-15-281786-7 pb

J L N O M K

Printed in Hong Kong

Bambolona, the baker's daughter, was angry.
Every day, summer, fall, winter, and spring,
she had to get up before the sun to bake the bread.
Then, piling the loaves on her head,
she went to deliver them.
But her work wasn't finished.
Rushing back to the bakery, she had to mix
the flour and salt and water and yeast
and set the dough to rise for tomorrow's bread.

"Don't forget," her father, the baker, would say,
"to make the cookies and bake the cakes.
  And remember, Bambolona, to clean up everything
  spic and span! I'm going now to see my friends."
  And off he would go to sit all day in the square
  of the little town in Calabria.

  One day Bambolona said, "Papa, there is too much
  work to do. I need some help."
"Get up earlier," her father said.
"But I get up now before the sun!" said Bambolona.
"And I'm the last one in town to get to bed."
"That's the way things are," her father said
  as he went out the door on his way to the square.
"And don't forget," he called back,
"you have a wedding cake to bake."

That did it.
Bambolona dusted the flour from her hands
and took off her apron.
"I'm going to *change* the way things are," she said.
"I'll go see Strega Nona.
She's so wise, she'll help me."

"I think I know how to help you,"
Strega Nona said after hearing Bambolona's sad tale.
"So many people come to me with their troubles.
I could certainly use some help.
Why not stay with me and I will teach you my magic."
"Oh, Strega Nona," said Bambolona, "thank you!"
"We'll start today," said Strega Nona.

Now, Big Anthony, who worked around the house
and in the garden for Strega Nona, was listening.
He was always listening to what other people
were talking about instead of working.
"Strega Nona!" he shouted, running into the house.
"Me too! Teach me your magic too!"

"Oh, Anthony," Strega Nona said with a smile,
"I can't do that. Why don't you go and milk the goat."
Now Big Anthony was the one who was angry!

"I'll show Strega Nona," he muttered. "I'll just go
and work for the baker, now that Bambolona has left."
Down the hill Big Anthony ran.

The baker hired him on the spot.
"The first thing you do is mix the dough,"
  the baker told Big Anthony.
"Put in this much flour, this much salt,
  this much water, and this much yeast."
He looked hard at Big Anthony's smiling face.
"Do you understand?
  The yeast makes the dough rise.
  Now mix it right away,
  and by the time I get back at six o'clock,
  the dough will be ready to make into loaves."
"*Sì Signore*—yes sir!" Big Anthony said.
The baker walked out the door and toward the square.

"I'll just look at everything first,"
said Big Anthony, poking around.

"Cookies!" He ate one, then another.

"Cakes!" He ate one, then another. Big Anthony ate them all.

In fact, he was still eating when the clock in the square struck four.

"*Mamma mia!*" said Big Anthony.
"I forgot to mix the dough. It won't rise in time.
Ah! I know. *The yeast makes the dough rise!*
I'll just put in a lot more of that,
and the dough will rise much faster!"

"I'll still have time for a nap,"
he said when he got through.
He sat down and promptly fell asleep.

What a sight the baker saw when he returned.

"OUT!" shouted the baker.

"What's the matter, Big Anthony?" asked Signora Rosa.
"The baker threw me out. Now I have no job,"
he answered. "And it's Strega Nona's fault.
I never would have left her house
if she had let me learn to be a *Strega.*"
"Silly goose," said Signora Rosa.
"Whoever heard of a man being a *Strega?*"

All of a sudden Big Anthony's eyes lit up,
and off he ran.

"To cure a headache, you must first fill the bowl
with water," Strega Nona was telling Bambolona.
"Next you add a few drops of olive oil.
Then you say these magic words . . ."
Knock, knock, knock.
Strega Nona went to the door.
"Oh, Strega Nona," said a tall girl, standing there.
"All my life I've wanted to learn your magic.
Will you teach me? Please?"
"*Santo Cielo*—dear me," said Strega Nona.

"What is your name, my girl?"
"Uh-h-h—Antonia," said the girl.
"Why do you want to learn my magic, Antonia?"
  Strega Nona asked.
"Oh, so that I can help people," said Antonia.
"Ever since I was a little girl,
  I've wanted to become a *Strega*."
"Ah, in that case," said Strega Nona,
"come right in. This is Bambolona.
  She is learning my magic, too."

Bambolona stared at Antonia and then at Strega Nona.
"How nice. Two girls to teach," Strega Nona said.
She smiled at Bambolona and then she began.
"To learn magic and practice it well," she said,
"you must learn to see *and* not to see. You must learn
to remember *and* to forget; to be still *and* to be busy.
But, mostly you must be faithful to your work.
Do you understand, my dears?"
"*Sì*—yes, Strega Nona," said Bambolona.
"No—*no*," said Antonia. "When are we going to
learn how to do the *magic* things?"

"In time," said Strega Nona.
"Now let's practice some of the magic words.
Repeat in the right order after me."
Soon Bambolona said all of them by heart.
Antonia kept mixing them up.

Bambolona learned the cure for headaches.   Antonia didn't.

Bambolona learned to make love potions.   Antonia didn't.

Bambolona learned how to get rid of warts.   Antonia didn't.

"Bambolona," said Strega Nona, "I think you are ready now to learn more powerful magic. This is a special book. It is very ancient and contains many magic secrets. Tomorrow we will begin with it."

"Oh *Grazie,* Strega Nona," said Bambolona.

"Me too, Strega Nona?" asked Antonia.

"Not yet, Antonia," said Strega Nona.

"You have other things to learn."

That night while everyone slept,
Antonia crept into Strega Nona's house.
"Bambolona thinks she's so smart," said Antonia.
"I'll just read that book tonight,
and tomorrow I'll surprise her *and* Strega Nona."

The next morning Antonia was looking very tired.
"Antonia," said Strega Nona, "watch and listen.
Come, Bambolona. We will start."
"Wait—wait," shouted Antonia. "I have a surprise.
I know some *real* magic. Watch me turn that iron kettle
into a golden one."
"Are you sure, Antonia?" said Strega Nona, frowning.
"Yes, oh yes," said Antonia, beginning to mutter some
strange-sounding words. But she stopped.
"Wait! I remember now." She began again.
"Be careful, Antonia," warned Bambolona.
"Magic can't be fooled with."
"I've got it now," Antonia said.

She muttered more words.
Suddenly there was a bright flash, some smelly smoke,
and the iron kettle
. . . was still *there!*

But Strega Nona wasn't.
Instead, where Strega Nona had been standing
was a nice fat TOAD.

"Now see what you've done!" cried Bambolona.
"Oh *no!*" shouted Antonia. "Oh help! Help,
somebody! Save Strega Nona! What have I done?"
"Strega Nona warned you to be careful with magic.
Now she's gone forever," Bambolona said.

"Strega Nona," wept Antonia, picking up the toad,
"forgive me, forgive me. Please, Bambolona, you're so
clever, you're so smart, please change her back again!
I promise I'll never play with magic again . . ."
"I can't change that toad into Strega Nona,"
said Bambolona. "But I *can* change Antonia into

. . . Big Anthony!"
Bambolona pulled off Antonia's kerchief and—
sure enough—there was Big Anthony!

"Oh, I'll never learn," howled Big Anthony,
"I'll never learn. Oh, Strega Nona—Strega Nona—
   what have I done to you?"
"Perhaps," said Bambolona, "if you really promise
   to never, ever play with magic again,
   that will bring Strega Nona back."

"Do you really think that would work?"
   said Big Anthony, sobbing.
"It's worth a try," said Bambolona.
   Big Anthony put down the toad.
   He closed his eyes tight
   and put his hand over his heart.
"I promise, I *really* promise,
   that as long as I live
   I will never play with magic again.
   Just please bring Strega Nona back."

There was another bright flash, some smelly smoke,
and *presto!* Strega Nona was back!
"Where am I?" said Strega Nona.
"Oh, I'm in my little house.
  Whatever happened to me?
  Hello, Bambolona. And, why, Big Anthony,
  what are *you* doing here? Where's sweet Antonia?"

"Tell her, Big Anthony," said Bambolona.
"Oh, Strega Nona," said Big Anthony,
   falling on his knees.
   He told Strega Nona what he had done.
   He was so busy crying and talking,
   he didn't see the nice fat toad
   hopping past him out the door.

"And so, Strega Nona, please," he said,
"if you take me back, I promise to be good.
I'll do all my chores and never play with magic again."

"All right, Anthony," said Strega Nona, smiling.
"But before you go back to work, change your clothes.
You're wearing Signora Rosa's nicest dress."